THE EXTRAORDINARY FILES

'The truth is inside us.
It is the only place where it can hide.'

nasen

NASEN House, 4/5 Amber Business Village, Amber Close,
Amington, Tamworth, Staffordshire B77 4RP

Rising Stars UK Ltd.
7 Hatchers Mews, Bermondsey Street, London SE1 3GS
www.risingstars-uk.com

Text © Rising Stars UK Ltd.
The right of Paul Blum to be identified as the author of this work has
been asserted by him in accordance with the Copyright, Design and
Patents Act 1988.

Published 2007
Reprinted 2008, 2011

Cover design: Button plc
Illustrator: Enzo Troiano
Text design and typesetting: pentacorbig
Publisher: Gill Budgell
Project management and editorial: Lesley Densham
Editor: Maoliosa Kelly
Editorial consultant: Lorraine Petersen

British Library Cataloguing in Publication Data.
A CIP record for this book is available from the British Library.

ISBN: 978 1 84680 182 2

Printed by Craft Print International Limited, Singapore

CHAPTER ONE

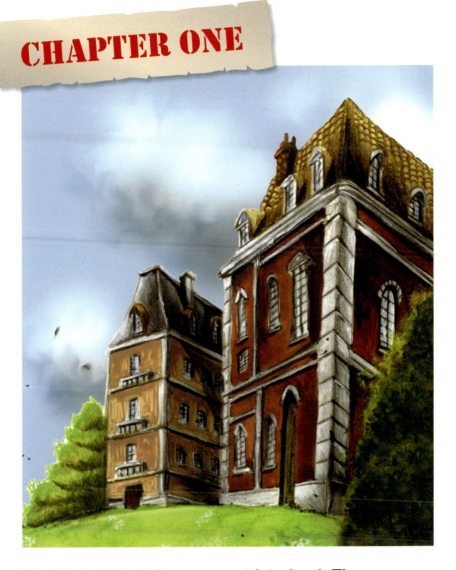

The big brick building was a girls' school. There were 200 girls, aged from eight to sixteen, at the school. All the girls were very rich.

One of the teachers was in the headmistress's office.
She was in trouble. She looked very frightened.
"I'm sorry," she said. "It will not happen again."

Madam Mellor, the headmistress, was sitting at her
desk. A puppet was sitting on her lap. The puppet was
a small man dressed in a black suit.

"Why did you ask a pupil a question in your lesson?" said the puppet.

"I'm sorry. I just forgot," sobbed the poor teacher.

"Sorry is not good enough. You did not do as you were told," the puppet replied.

"Kneel down, Miss Baker," the puppet said.

Two guards pushed her down.

"Please, please, let me go," screamed Miss Baker.

The puppet grabbed her. His glass eyes gleamed. There was no mercy in them.

CHAPTER TWO

Vauxhall London MI5 Headquarters

Commander Watson called Agent Parker into his office.

"Are you good at DIY?" he asked.

"What a strange question," thought Parker.

"You are going to become a painter," said Watson, smiling. "We'll give you some basic training."

"So I'm going under cover?" Parker asked.

Watson nodded. He looked out of the window. He had a wonderful view of the River Thames from his office in the MI5 building.

Then he said, "I want you to do a little detective work at Greenock School in Kent. Something strange is going on there. Three girls and a teacher have disappeared. At the same time, Madam Mellor, the headmistress has been getting the best exam results in the country. Every girl got full marks in everything!"

"Catching schools that cheat in exams is not really Secret Service work," Parker said.

"You are right, Agent. But we think there is more to it than a little bit of cheating. We need information about this school quickly and you are our man."

"Don't you think I'll stick out in a girls' school?" Parker asked.

"Not if you are just painting the walls. And while you are up ladders you'll be getting information."

Watson handed him a paint roller.

"This handy little machine can hear conversations through walls that are ten feet thick."

"Cool," said Parker, looking at it.

"It's a very expensive machine, Agent Parker.
Take good care of it," the commander said. "Never dip
it in a can of paint!"

"No, Sir," replied Parker.

Commander Watson showed him out.

"Will Agent Turnbull be working with me?" Parker asked.

"Yes. When we have something to go on."

CHAPTER THREE

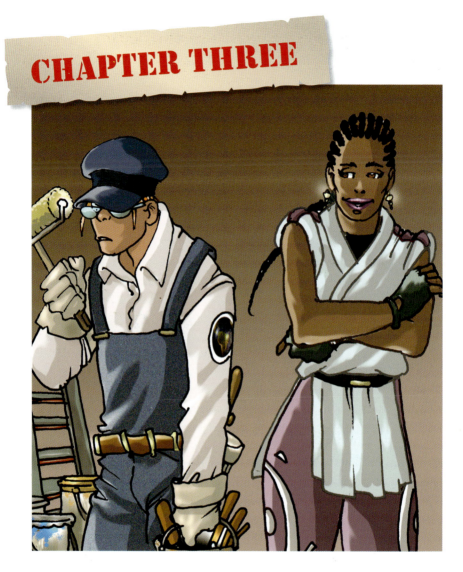

Parker got ready to go under cover.

"Fancy asking you of all people to be a painter," laughed Turnbull. "They should see the state of your flat!"

"Perhaps I'll be good at it," said Parker.

When he arrived at Greenock School, it was very quiet. At break time the 200 girls came out to the playground. They just walked about. Nobody laughed or smiled. When the teacher rang the bell they went back inside without a sound.

Nobody gave him a second look. Parker started to relax. Perhaps he would be able to get on with the painting job after all.

Madam Mellor, the headmistress, asked him to paint the main school building first.

He started to paint. It was a hot, sunny day but all the classroom windows were shut. In fact, they had wooden shutters and metal bars across them.

Parker could not see anything that was going on in the classrooms, but he could hear everything. The girls were so good. They did what they were told to do.

The teacher did not get cross with the pupils. The pupils did not get cross with each other.

"Something is not right here," thought Parker. All he could hear was the teacher saying things and the girls repeating them. Nobody asked or answered a question. They just repeated things, again and again. Parker thought it was spooky.

On the third day, Parker wanted to see a lesson. He made a hole in one of the windows and peeped in.

The class had two teachers – a man and a woman. The man was very small.

"The class is being taught by a puppet!" he said.

As he pulled away in shock, the ladder wobbled.

"Mr Parker, are you all right?" Madam Mellor called up to him. "You nearly fell off."

"I'm fine, Headmistress," said Parker.

He picked up the nearest paint roller and dipped it in the pot. "I'm fine, really fine," he said, brushing madly. Madam Mellor looked at him strangely but she didn't say anything.

When she had gone, Parker looked at his paint roller and groaned. The Secret Service operation was at an end. The expensive machine that could hear a whisper through a ten foot wall was destroyed.

"Oh no, Watson is going to kill me," he said.

Parker put the ladder into his van. He went to Madam Mellor's office to say he was leaving. The door was open. He heard angry voices shouting. Madam Mellor was shouting at the puppet on her hand.

"You are doing terrible things to my school," she shouted. "It must stop!"

"Just do as you are told," the puppet shouted back.

The headmistress tried to throw the puppet away but he held onto her hand.

"It is time to get a new leader of this school," the puppet said coldly. "You must go!"

"Why did I let you do this to my pupils? They look so sad now," sobbed the headmistress.

The puppet laughed.

"*Your* pupils," he sneered. "They are *my* pupils now! The future is deep hypnosis. The future is puppets."

Parker had seen enough. He left Greenock School and went back to London.

17

CHAPTER FOUR

Vauxhall London MI5 Headquarters

"Sit down, Agent Turnbull," said Commander Watson. "This is Chief Commander Williams."

Turnbull shook hands with Belinda Williams. She was in charge of the whole of MI5.

"I've heard a lot about you," said Chief Commander Williams. "You are one of our best young agents."

"Thank you, Chief Commander," said Turnbull, blushing.

"That is why we are putting you on this difficult case."

"With my partner Agent Parker?' asked Turnbull.

"He will be on the case later," she said.

"So what do I have to do?"

19

"You are going to become headmistress of Greenock Girls' School."

"Headmistress? I haven't been in a school in years."

"You'll be fine," said the Chief Commander. "You are a bright girl. You will learn quickly."

"Is it the school where the puppets are hypnotising the teachers and the pupils?" Turnbull asked.

"It is. We want to find out as much as we can about this school," said Commander Watson.

"The last headmistress disappeared!" said Turnbull.

"I would be lying to you if I said there was no danger," said Watson. "But you will have contact with headquarters at all times. A back-up team can get you out very quickly if the puppets turn nasty."

"Lots of teachers will want this job. It is one of the best schools in the country," she said.

"Yes they will. We will make sure that they pick you," said Chief Commander Williams, smiling at her.

"How?" asked Turnbull.

"Listen Laura, sometimes you just have to do as you are told. The less you know, the better," said Williams.

In no time they were standing beside the lift.

"Good luck, Laura," said Chief Commander Williams.

"Thanks."

"Wait at home for your orders. And don't talk to anybody!"

"Not even Parker?" said Turnbull.

"Not even Parker. We'll tell him what is happening," she said, putting her hand on Turnbull's shoulder.

"Don't worry. Just go home and relax."

CHAPTER FIVE

Turnbull went home.
She was not happy.
She smelled a rat.
This was not the first
time her bosses had
been up to tricks.

Had they told her
only part of the truth?
She walked up and
down the flat.
What should she do?
Then she picked up
the phone.

Parker came straight over.

"They are putting you in danger," he said.

"What can I do?" she said. "I have to obey my orders."

Parker looked in his bag. He pulled out a strange machine. "Fix this to your teeth," he said.

"Are you mad?"

"If you are in danger, bite into this and it will give out an emergency signal. I will come at once."

"But MI5 are watching me every second of the day," she said.

"Yes, tell me about it," he said grimly. "Come on, Turnbull. Pigs could fly. You phoned me because you don't trust them. You have already disobeyed an order haven't you?"

She nodded her head.

"So what do you have to lose? Bite it and I'll be there."

Suddenly she felt happy. She squeezed his hand.

"You're a good friend, Robert," she said.

As he turned to go, she pulled him back. She kissed him on the cheek.

"Robert, I don't know what I would do without you," she said.

He tried to say something but he was too shy. He hurried off, without looking back at her.

CHAPTER SIX

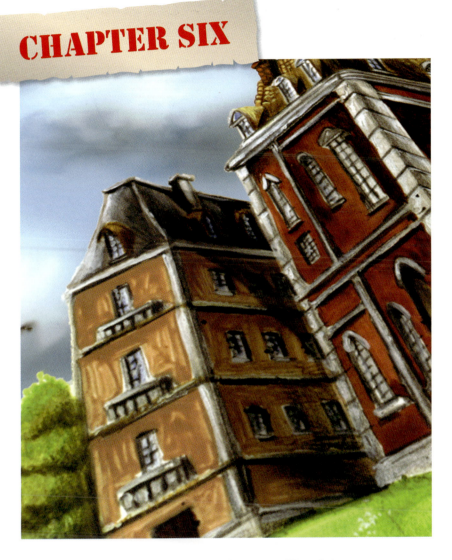

Turnbull went to Greenock School. She felt nervous. She had read her orders many times. Especially the bit about how to stop somebody from hypnotising you.

A guard showed her into the headmistress's office.

Sitting at a long table was a woman holding a puppet on her arm. It was the same puppet that Parker had told her about.

"Welcome to Greenock Girls' School, Miss Turnbull," said the puppet.

Turnbull nodded and smiled.

"I am Dr Mania. I am the chief advisor to the Head. The person holding me is my secretary Miss Brown."

Turnbull nodded again. She tried not to look surprised.

Dr Mania smiled. "Don't look so worried Miss Turnbull you will soon understand everything. Come and meet the other teachers."

One by one, she met the other puppets.

"And now, Miss Turnbull, we have some questions to ask you. Why do you want to be Head of this School?"

Turnbull felt many glassy eyes turn to look at her. She felt very nervous.

"I . . . er . . . um. I have always wanted to help young people to learn," she said.

The puppet smiled.

"So do we, Miss Turnbull. That is why you must watch my eyes and repeat some words after me."

"I don't understand. I . . ." she said.

"Just close your eyes and repeat these words after me."

She closed her eyes.

"I promise to obey the commands of the great one. I must never think for myself."

She repeated the words again and again. So did the other puppets. Their voices hit her like waves of water on a beach. In the end they took over her mind.

After five minutes of chanting, Dr Mania held up his plastic hand. All the puppets stopped. Only Turnbull went on talking in the silent room. Dr Mania smiled.

"She is ours. Welcome to the new headmistress of Greenock School."

CHAPTER SEVEN

Parker went back to work at the school.
He had seen Turnbull come and go but he
had not been able to speak to her. Her eyes
looked big and glassy. Parker got more and
more worried. "She's been hypnotised.
So much for our Secret Service!" he thought.

On the third morning, Parker wanted to see
Headmistress Turnbull teach a class. He made
a small hole in the window frame and looked
through it. Turnbull was teaching a maths lesson.
She had a puppet on the end of her arm. Turnbull
was talking and the puppet was writing notes in
a little book.

"We will do our five times table," Turnbull said.
"One times five is five."

"One times five is five," repeated the girls.

"Two times five is ten."

Parker turned away. He felt sick. He knew that his partner was lost. Parker watched and waited. He made a careful plan. Everyday he watched the headmistress's movements, until he got to know Turnbull's teaching timetable by heart.

Finally, when he was sure that there was nobody watching he stopped her as she walked between lessons.

"Laura, it's me," he whispered.

She kept on walking.

"Laura. It's Robert Parker, your partner."

She looked at him strangely. He grabbed her by the shoulders.

"Laura – you know me, don't you?"

"An adjective is a describing word," she replied.

"Laura, Laura. You are a secret service agent, remember?"

"A verb is an action word."

He shook her but it made no difference. He had one last trick to play.

SNAP!

He snapped his fingers. Turnbull blinked. She was no longer hypnotised.

"It works every time!" he laughed.

"Where am I?" she asked.

"You are at Greenock School for Girls. You are the headmistress. You are on the way to your next lesson."

"Oh yes, I remember now," Turnbull replied.

"And you've been hypnotised by the puppet who is running this place. Hopefully you're better now. It's been very boring talking to you lately."

Suddenly they heard footsteps. Parker pulled Turnbull into a hedge. Dr Mania and his secretary went past them. The puppet was moving his head from side to side.

"I think he is looking for me," Turnbull whispered. "I'm late for my history lesson."

33

CHAPTER EIGHT

The class was silent when she got there. She told the girls about the women who had fought to get the vote. Suddenly Dr Mania, his secretary and the security guards burst into the room. Dr Mania came up to her desk and sat on her table.

Turnbull went on with the lesson.

"So the women tied themselves to gates because they were so angry . . ."

"Two times two is four," said the puppet.

"They wanted the same freedom as men," Turnbull went on, not looking at him.

"Three times two is six. Four times two is eight," snapped the puppet.

"This is a history lesson," said Turnbull, glaring at Dr Mania.

"Five times two is ten, six times two is twelve," he said.

"Do you mind? I'm teaching."

"I promise to obey the commands of the great one," he screamed at her.

"Get out of my classroom at once!" she shouted back.

The puppet went red with anger.

"Guards! Seize her!" he screamed.

They dragged Turnbull to the swimming pool.

"Get off me," she shouted. "I'm the headmistress."

The girls from the school started screaming with excitement.

"Check her pockets," Dr Mania said. "We don't want her making contact with Painter Parker."

"What are you doing? Leave me alone," she said.

They took her mobile away. They made her sit on the diving board. They tied her hands behind her back. This was an emergency. She bit into her tooth. Surely Chief Commander Williams and the back-up team would be there immediately. But if they didn't, then Parker would get the alarm.

"Hurry up, Parker," she whispered. "I haven't got long to live."

Dr Mania waved his plastic hand. The girls stopped screaming.

"Pupils of Greenock School, your headmistress is not what she seems. Miss Turnbull is in fact Agent Turnbull. She works for the Secret Service. She has come here to stop you from learning your lessons. She wants you to go back to learning the old way. She wants you to think for yourselves."

All the girls hissed.

Dr Mania pointed to Turnbull.

"What should we do to her?"

"Kill her, kill her, kill her!" shouted the girls.

The puppet smiled. "Open the gates," he said, pointing at the pool.

Turnbull looked down. She saw a large fin in the water. It was a shark. Turnbull panicked. She tried to get away. Dr Mania and the puppets laughed at her.

"I don't think so, Agent Turnbull," sneered the puppet. "I hope you like swimming. Untie her."

Turnbull tried to look brave but she was very frightened.

"Guards, throw her in," shouted the puppet.

Suddenly the girls screamed. A man in a wetsuit had jumped into the pool. The girls gasped as the shark swam towards him. The man dived under the water and pushed the shark away from him. Then the man shot a dart in its side.

Dr Mania was shocked. "Who is it? Who is this man? I was told there would be no MI5," the puppet shouted.

Turnbull saw her chance and punched the secretary in the face. She fell to the ground and Turnbull pulled the glove puppet off her hand.

"Help, help, help me," Dr Mania screamed.

"You are under arrest," Turnbull said to the puppet.

The girls screamed again. 20 masked men suddenly appeared. They grabbed all the puppets and their secretaries. One pulled the diver out of the pool. Three surrounded Turnbull.

"It's OK, Agent Turnbull. We are the back-up team. You're in safe hands," one of them said.

"But I've arrested Dr Mania."

"Don't worry. We'll take care of him now."

They took Dr Mania out of her hands. When she turned round, all the puppets had gone.

CHAPTER NINE

Vauxhall London M15 Headquarters

Parker and Turnbull were in the gym.

"What happened to Dr Mania and his secretary?" asked Turnbull. "I hope they are in jail."

"They are somewhere in this building," said Parker. "The Secret Service is very interested in the energy link between puppet and puppet master."

In a sudden fit of temper, Turnbull threw her badge across the floor.

"There is no right or wrong in this place," she said. "That Dr Mania wanted to kill me. He had it all planned. He knew about MI5 and he didn't think they would rescue me. He was shocked when you turned up."

Parker nodded his head in agreement.

"If MI5 discover you have secret powers, then you can get away with murder," Parker said sadly.

"I am fed up with this organisation," Turnbull said. "I want out of it!"

Parker looked at his feet. There was nothing he could say. Everything she said was true. But he had a funny feeling that leaving MI5 would be difficult for people who knew too much.

GLOSSARY OF TERMS

hypnotised a trance-like state where the person obeys orders and does not think for himself

MI5 government department responsible for national security

pigs could fly something very unlikely to happen

Secret Service Government Intelligence Department

to smell a rat to be suspicious that something is wrong

under cover on a secret operation

QUIZ

1 What is the name of the school?

2 What is the name of the headmistress?

3 Who is in control of the school?

4 What does Commander Watson give Agent Parker?

5 Who is Belinda Williams?

6 What does the puppet do to Agent Turnbull at the interview?

7 What is the name of the puppet?

8 What was in the swimming pool?

9 How many masked men appeared?

10 Who took Dr Mania away?

ABOUT THE AUTHOR

Paul Blum has taught for over twenty years in London inner-city schools.

I wrote The Extraordinary Files for my pupils so they've been tested by some fierce critics (you!). That's why I know you'll enjoy reading them.

I've made the stories edgy in terms of character and content and I've written them using the kind of fast-paced dialogue you'll recognise from television soaps. I hope you'll find The Extraordinary Files an interesting and easy-to-read collection of stories.

ANSWERS TO QUIZ

1 Greenock School

2 Madam Mellor

3 The puppets

4 A listening device disguised as a paint roller

5 Chief Commander of MI5

6 Hypnotise her

7 Dr Mania

8 A shark

9 20

10 The masked men